Grace-Ella

PIXIE PANDEMONIUM

First published in 2021 by Firefly Press
25 Gabalfa Road, Llandaff North, Cardiff, CF14 2JJ
www.fireflypress.co.uk

A CIP catalogue record of this book
is available from the British Library.

1 3 5 7 9 8 6 4 2

ISBN 9781913102623
ebook ISBN 9781913102630

This book has been published with the support of the Books Council of Wales.

Designed by Claire Brisley.

Printed and bound by CPI Group, UK.

Grace-Ella

PIXIE PANDEMONIUM

Sharon Marie Jones

Illustrated by
Adriana J Puglisi

To Mam

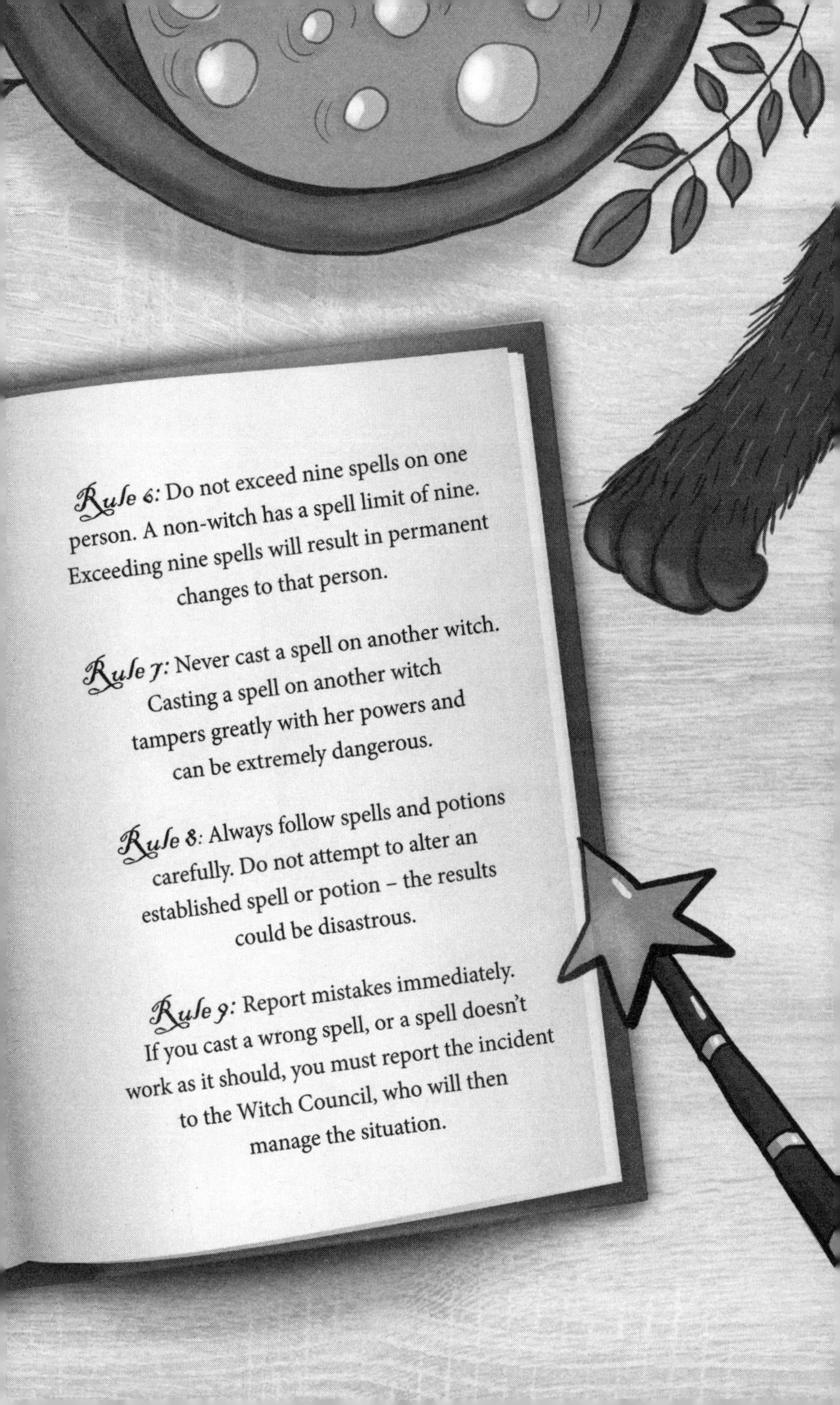
Rule 6: Do not exceed nine spells on one person. A non-witch has a spell limit of nine. Exceeding nine spells will result in permanent changes to that person.
Rule 7: Never cast a spell on another witch. Casting a spell on another witch tampers greatly with her powers and can be extremely dangerous.
Rule 8: Always follow spells and potions carefully. Do not attempt to alter an established spell or potion – the results could be disastrous.
Rule 9: Report mistakes immediately. If you cast a wrong spell, or a spell doesn't work as it should, you must report the incident to the Witch Council, who will then manage the situation.

Contents

Grace-Ella's Witch Kit

When Grace-Ella became a witch, these are all the things she was sent by the Witch Council to help her train. All witches must follow the Nine Golden Rules or they could lose their magic.

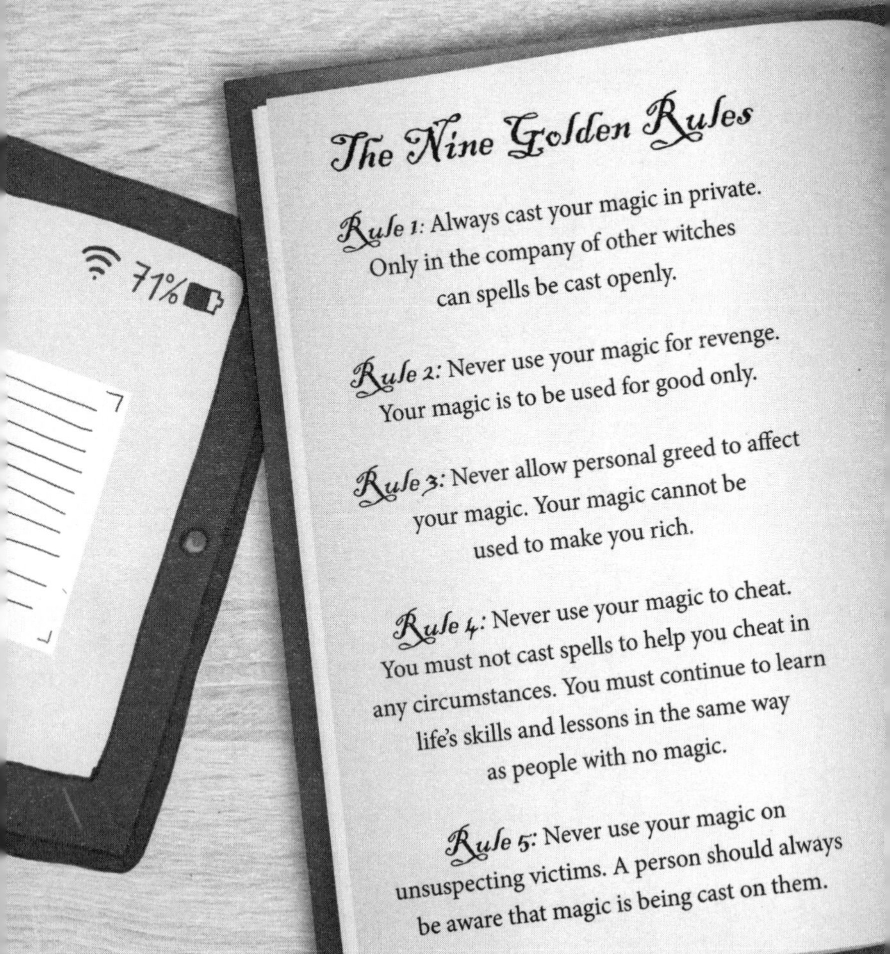

Chapter One

Things that Go Bump in the Night

It was nine o'clock on Friday night and after enjoying a bubbly bath and a hot chocolate topped with a melting marshmallow mountain, Grace-Ella flopped onto her bed.

'This has been the best week ever,' she said with a loud yawn.

Grace-Ella had just returned from Witch Camp. She had learned new spells and potions, and even how to fly on a broomstick. She was now the proud owner of her very own magical plant, the Stinging Screamer. Its star-shaped flowers could whisper secret spells.

'I can't wait to tell Bedwyr and Fflur all about our Witch Camp adventure,' she said, snuggling down under the duvet.

Her cat, Mr Whiskins, replied with a

gentle, purring snore, and soon Grace-Ella's eyes drifted closed.

Grace-Ella stirred. It was inky dark but something had woken her.

Rustle, rustle...

She sat upright and rubbed her eyes. Mr Whiskins was fast asleep at the foot of her bed, his whiskers twitching as he dreamed.

Thud, thump...

She switched on the string of star lights hanging above her headboard and squinted around her room.

'Mr Whiskins,' she whispered, nudging him with her foot. 'Are you awake?'

'No, I am very much asleep,' mumbled Mr Whiskins, who was not a cat who liked to be woken up in the middle of the pitch-dark night.

'Can you hear something?' she asked.

'Yes, you,' he muttered.

Shuffle, scuffle...

'There! Did you hear it? I think it's coming from over in the corner.'

With a sleepy sigh, Mr Whiskins stretched his front legs, kneaded his paws and padded up the bed. They peered into the corner of the room.

On the floor was Grace-Ella's unpacked rucksack from Witch Camp. It was moving.

The zip was slowly opening.

Zzziiippp...

Out of the opening rucksack came a pointy, green hat with a jingly bell, followed by two twinkling eyes, a snub nose and a mischievous grin. Grace-Ella gawped. Standing in the middle of her bedroom was Buddy Whiffleflip, the forest pixie from Witch Camp!

'How...? What...? When...?' she spluttered.

'Please tell me this isn't happening,' groaned Mr Whiskins, covering his eyes with his front paws.

Buddy Whiffleflip reached up high then touched his toes. 'I must have dozed off,' he

said, hopping up onto the bed.

Mr Whiskins burrowed under the pillow.

'What are you doing here?' asked a still stunned Grace-Ella.

'Pixie work is tremendously tiring, so I'm here for a holiday,' Buddy replied. He started counting off his daily must-do list. 'Forest patrol, write a scroll, dust-mixing, tidying, mischief-making. Buzzy-busy from the crow's-caw to owls-out.'

Grace-Ella didn't know what to say but she couldn't help feeling a fizzle of excitement. There was a runaway pixie sitting on her bed! 'How did you get into my rucksack? I didn't see you in there when I was packing.'

'You should never leave your bag alone in the middle of a magical forest. You never know what may be lurking nearby. A whispering willow fairy could have fluttered in and that would have been terribly troublesome for you.'

Grace-Ella frowned. She hadn't left her rucksack in the forest. She'd been carrying it the whole time … until she had stopped with Penelope Pendle, head of the Witch Council, who let her dig up her Stinging Screamer. She had put her rucksack down so that she could pull the plant from the ground. That's when Buddy must have sneaked in.

This was an official pixie predicament.

'Well, you can't just turn up uninvited,' Mr Whiskins was saying, coming out from under the pillow. 'You'll have to go straight back to the forest.'

'You cats can be so *grumpsome*,' huffed Buddy. 'I think it's up to Grace-Ella to decide if I can stay.'

Two pairs of eyes stared at Grace-Ella:

one pair wide and twinkling, the other narrow and glowering. What was she going to do? Her mam would definitely not approve of having a pixie as a guest. And her dad … well, he probably wouldn't notice.

No, she couldn't have a forest pixie staying with them. She would have to send a message to Penelope Pendle to come and collect him.

But it would be fun and not really any bother, just for a short while.

'Ummm … I suppose it would be OK … only for a few days.'

'Yippee!' Buddy squealed and somersaulted into the air.

Mr Whiskins slowly shook his head, as if Grace-Ella had just made the biggest mistake of her entire life.

'But you'll have to do what I say,' she

warned. 'I can't let Mam find out you're here or you'll be back in the forest faster than a finger-click.'

'I'll be on my best behaviour,' said Buddy, standing as still and as tall as a pixie could possibly be.

'Right, well it's the middle of the night so we should all be asleep.'

'Now that is a good idea,' said Mr Whiskins. 'Hopefully we'll wake up in the morning and all this will have been a bad dream.'

'I'm too excited to sleep,' said Buddy, flipping and flying.

'If you're going to stay here, you'll have to follow my rules,' said Grace-Ella in her strictest voice. 'And the first rule is that night-time is for sleeping. So let's settle down and go to sleep.'

Buddy begrudgingly stopped bouncing

and bundled himself next to Mr Whiskins.

'I am not a fluffy blanket,' the cat growled, shuffling to the edge of the bed.

Buddy wiggled and wriggled then kicked out his legs, striking Mr Whiskins and sending him with a bump to the floor.

'Goodnight, Buddy, sleep tight.' Grace-Ella couldn't stop smiling as she thought of the fun they would have over the next few days.

Mr Whiskins, on the other hand, was not at all happy, as he curled up under the bed grumbling about pesky pixies.

Chapter Two
Pixie-promise

The following morning Grace-Ella was woken up far too early for a Saturday by a very wide-awake pixie.

'Open your eyes and rub your nose,
Stretch up high then tickle your toes,
Wiggle and giggle and hop out of bed,
Wakey-wakey sleepyhead!'

Buddy blew a puff of golden pixie dust onto Grace-Ella. Rocketing up, she hopped and bopped around her room before tumbling back onto her bed.

'That's one way ... to get me up ... in the morning,' she said, gasping for breath.

Mr Whiskins poked his head out from under the bed. 'I don't suppose you're celebrating because the pixie problem has vanished?'

'And a very good morning to you too,' said Buddy, tipping topsy-turvy over the side of the bed.

'I can most definitely see nothing good about this morning,' answered Mr Whiskins, batting his paw at Buddy, who was dangling in front of his face.

'Now that everyone's awake, it must be time for breakfast,' said Buddy.

'Oh!' exclaimed Grace-Ella. 'I have no idea what pixies eat. And the dishes in the house will be far too big for you.'

'I am approximately twenty acorns high on the pixie measuring chart,' announced Buddy, stretching to his full height.

Grace-Ella rummaged through the wooden chest of old toys. She pulled out a pretty, patterned miniature china tea set.

'I've never played with it but it's the perfect size for a pixie.' She set the little tea set out on her rug. 'Right, what would you like for breakfast?'

'Honey-dipped bread with a refreshing cup of morning dew, please.' Buddy whipped a crisp, white handkerchief from his pocket and tucked it under his chin.

'I'll be back in a dash,' said Grace-Ella.

Grace-Ella's mam, Mrs Bevin, was very surprised to see her daughter in the kitchen so early.

'I thought you would have had a lovely lie-in,' she said, 'especially after being at Witch Camp all week.'

'But it's a beautiful morning, the birds are singing and I'm just going for a walk round the garden to breathe in the fresh air.'

Grace-Ella skipped out through the back door, leaving Mrs Bevin staring open-mouthed. Grace-Ella was not an early riser and was definitely not one for skipping round the garden. It seemed being a witch was having a very positive effect on her, which pleased Mrs Bevin immensely.

Coming back in, Grace-Ella was relieved that her mam had left the kitchen. She didn't want to have to explain why she was carrying a miniature cup of morning dew. She cut some bread into small chunks and grabbed a pot of honey from the cupboard.

'Breakfast is served,' she said, as she walked back into her bedroom.

'Yum-scrum,' said Buddy. He dipped a chunk of bread into a dollop of sticky honey.

Mr Whiskins coughed ... then coughed again.

'Kippers! I forgot your breakfast kippers,' blurted Grace-Ella, spraying crumbs of bread onto the rug.

'You've very clearly been pixie-possessed.' With a swish of his tail, Mr Whiskins stalked out of the room.

'Oh dear, I'll have to make it up to him later with his favourite catnip treat.'

Once breakfast had been devoured, Buddy sprinkled some golden pixie dust over the dishes.

'Wishy-washy, soak and scrub,
Clear away this breakfast grub,
Pat and dry, all nice and clean,
Dirty dishes sparkle and gleam.'

Grace-Ella grinned as the dishes rattled and clattered in a lather of soapy suds, before stacking themselves neat and shiny on the now crumb-free rug. Having Buddy to stay was proving to be a brilliant decision.

In the summer house at the bottom of the garden, Grace-Ella set about sorting her new potion ingredients from Witch Camp. Once they were stored alphabetically on the shelves, she decided to brew some Lullaby Lavender Lemonade. She had a feeling that it wasn't going to be easy to get an excitable pixie to bed at night, so a cup of her magical lemonade might be very helpful.

Mr Whiskins was still sulking over

the forgotten kippers. So it was up to Buddy to help Grace-Ella with her potion ingredients.

'You have to promise not to sprinkle any pixie dust into the cauldron. *Rule 8: Always follow spells and potions carefully*,' said Grace-Ella, reciting one of the Nine Golden Rules set by the Witch Council.

'Pixie-promise,' replied Buddy, linking his two little fingers and wiggling his thumbs.

'Right ... I need six sprigs of lavender, seven stalks of sleepy grass, a sprinkle of sage, a ladle of lemon juice and nine nightingale feathers.'

In a whirl of green, Buddy whipped up the ingredients lightning-quick.

'Lastly, I need to wink forty times.'

She stirred the potion with a wooden spoon and said the magic words.

Lavender, lemon and purple delight,
Mix up together all bubbly and bright,
Nightingale sing me a sweet lullaby,
Drift off to dream with a soft sleepy sigh.'

Violet-coloured bubbles floated out of the cauldron. Each bubble burst with a musical note, filling the air with a soothing melody. Grace-Ella carefully poured the potion into a bottle. Just as she was pushing the cork stopper in, the door of the summer house flew open. Her friend Bedwyr bundled in, wearing his full bug-busting gear.

'So come on, I want to hear all about Witch Camp. Did you see any magic bugs? Did anyone eat a poisonous plant? Did you fly on a broomstick? Did anyone fall from the sky?'

'Take a breath!' Grace-Ella laughed. 'I'll tell you all about it in a minute. First, I want you to meet someone, but you have to promise not to tell anybody.'

'Okay, I promise,' replied Bedwyr. He looked eagerly around the summer house.

'Pixie-promise?' asked Grace-Ella, linking her two little fingers and wiggling her thumbs.

'Uh … pixie-promise…' Bedwyr copied her.

'Bedwyr, meet Buddy Whiffleflip.'

Buddy stepped out from behind the cauldron. 'Charmed to meet you,' he said, with his customary regal bow.

'Buddy's a forest pixie and has come here on his holiday,' explained Grace-Ella.

'Oh my giddy goose! There's a real-life pixie standing in front of me. An actual real … life … PIXIE!'

'Great,' said Mr Whiskins, who was watching from the open door. 'Another one pixie-possessed.'

Chapter Three
Bugtastic!

Being bonkers about bugs, Bedwyr wanted to ask Buddy all about magical bugs.

'I bet there are billions in your forest,' he said, his eyes big and bright.

'They're everywhere,' replied Buddy.

Bedwyr lunged into his bug-bag and pulled out a notebook and pencil.

'Tell me all about them so I can write everything down in my bug-book.'

Buddy was enjoying Bedwyr's attention and clearly feeling very important. Grace-Ella sat down next to them. She was always excited to talk about magic things. Even Mr Whiskins had strolled in but was pretending to be not at all interested by playing with a ball of string.

'Magical bugs have very special work to

do,' explained Buddy. 'There are the mail-snails and their slow service. Last week I received a postcard from my friend, Herbie Tiggletwig, that he'd sent from his holiday in Misty Ash Forest two years ago! They drag their post satchels behind them in their sticky snail-trails. You can't even read the post when it finally arrives as it's all smudgy.'

'Snail mail! There's actually such a thing as snail mail!' whooped Bedwyr, scribbling frantically in his bug-book.

'And a very slow service it is too,' Buddy continued. 'The blustering blowflies will be hibernating soon, once they've blown all the leaves from the trees. We won't see them again until next autumn. There are map-winged moths which are very helpful if you stray from the path and get lost.'

'Moths with map-wings? This is

bugtastic! You have to take me to a magic forest.'

'If I could I would,' said Grace-Ella. 'But only those of us with magic at the tips of our fingers can find the secret way into a magical forest.'

'It's so unfair. I could be the world's most famous bugologist. A museum would be built especially for me: "Bedwyr's Bugarium". And people from all over the world would come and listen to me talk about bugs.'

'He gets carried away like a hot-air balloon,' mumbled Mr Whiskins, as he tried to untangle himself from the ball of string.

Buddy told them all about the bumbling bees buzzing around the forest, bumping into everything and bumbling their apologies. He described the bog beetles, the ladybugs and the flashing fireflies that light up the forest at night.

'My favourite are the majestic dragonflies,' he said. 'It's lucky that they spend most of their time hovering over streams, especially in winter when they're most likely to catch a cold. You don't want to be standing in front of a dragonfly when it sneezes a fiery flame.'

'My favourite bug is the assassin bug, although I haven't found one yet. Are there any in your forest?' asked Bedwyr. 'Don't tell me, they wait in ambush for their enemies with their spears fastened to their backs.'

'Their job is to combat critter-crime,' explained Buddy. 'But I am an excellent forest-patroller so there is barely a *sniffet* of bad bug behaviour in my forest. Our assassin bugs spend most of their time admiring their spear-sharp beaks in droplets of dew.'

'But my *Bug Encyclopaedia* says that the assassin bug is deadly. I read that it's a vicious hunter that sucks blood from its victims.'

'Well, that's just *feathersome* flimflam,' stated Buddy.

'Magical bugs behave very differently

from ordinary bugs,' clarified Grace-Ella. 'I'll try to find a *Magical Bug Encyclopaedia* for you. Maybe there's one in Dad's bookshop. I wish I'd had time to meet more of the magical bugs when I was at Witch Camp. I'd love to see the ladybugs strolling around with their parasols and watch the tricky ticks perform a magic show.'

'I'll give you a full forest tour next time you come and introduce you to everyone,' said Buddy.

'Witches have the best fun,' sighed Bedwyr.

The weekend passed with no pixie problems. Buddy was mostly well-behaved and a cup of Lullaby Lavender Lemonade at bedtime had him snoring soundly all night. Mr Whiskins got over the forgotten kippers and was soon capering about with Buddy.

A sprinkling of pixie dust on the horse-chestnut tree made it start catapulting conkers in all directions, and the sprightly pair pounced and bounced around the garden dodging the prickly missiles.

At bedtime on Sunday, Grace-Ella explained to Buddy that she had to go to school the following day. 'It'll be best if you stay at home with Mr Whiskins. You'd only have to stay hidden in my bag all day.'

'But I've never been to school. Please can I come with you? Pixie-please?'

Grace-Ella hesitated. What would Buddy get up to at home, left alone, if he got bored?

'I suppose you can come if you pixie-promise to stay in my bag. I can't have any teachers seeing you. And I definitely can't let Amelia see you. She's forever trying to get me into trouble. If she finds out I have a pixie hiding in my bag, she'll have you plonked on Mrs Nag's desk and me booted out of the school in a bat's blink.'

'Hmph! She sounds like a miserable old meanie. You should use your magic to teach her a lesson.'

'I wish I could,' said Grace-Ella with a sigh. 'But I have to follow the Nine Golden Rules, and Rule 2 says that I must never use my magic for revenge.'

'Hmm ... those rules are for witches, not for pixies...'

'No, Buddy. You have to pixie-promise to stay hidden in my bag. I can't have you causing chaos at school.'

'Okay, pixie-promise.'

Grace-Ella turned to her desk to sort out her school books. She didn't notice that Buddy didn't link his little fingers and wiggle his thumbs, but crossed his fingers behind his back. He was very fond of Grace-Ella and didn't like the sound of anyone being horrible to her. A pixie was a true and faithful friend, so he wasn't going to stay hidden if Grace-Ella was in trouble.

Chapter Four
Apple Scrumping

With Buddy secretly tucked away in her bag, Grace-Ella set off for school on Monday morning. She waved goodbye to her dad as he drove off, then walked up the tree-lined driveway of St Winifred's Girls' School.

'You have to stay still and not make a sound,' she whispered to Buddy. 'When it's break time, you can come out and meet my friend, Fflur.'

After lining up, she hung her bag on her peg and went to class.

'Good morning,' trilled Mrs Nag. 'Now, as we all know, the end of term is looming and the Christmas holidays will soon be here ... which means it's time for our end of term tests.'

Grace-Ella groaned. She hated tests. She never got full marks and always had to have extra homework.

'Our annual Christmas Fair will be held next Friday,' continued Mrs Nag. 'This year, I have a special project for you all. In pairs, you will have a stall each at the fair and you'll be designing and making a Christmas product to sell. The money from your sales will be added to the school's Fundraising Flowerpot. Your stalls will be judged and the winning stall will choose this year's charity and be awarded our new trophy, "Excellent Entrepreneur". You'll be judged on creativity, quality and presentation.'

The classroom filled with excited chatter. It was clear from the faraway look on Amelia's face that she was already dreaming about holding up the new trophy and giving a thank-you speech.

'But right now, I want you to switch on your thinking and concentration for your maths test. Move to sit at the ends of your tables please, so that you can't copy from your neighbour. What do we say at St Winifred's?'

'Copying is cheating, as we all know. It won't help us learn or develop and grow,' chorused the class.

The bell for break time couldn't come soon enough for Grace-Ella.

'Follow me,' she whispered to Fflur as they walked out of the classroom.

Snatching her bag from her peg she hurried towards the school garden.

Running after her, Fflur puffed, 'What's the rush?'

'You'll see.'

They sat on a bench, hidden by apple trees. Grace-Ella opened her bag. 'You can come out now.'

'Yippee!' Buddy jumped out.

Fflur clasped a hand over her mouth to stifle a scream. Her eyes seemed to pop right out of their sockets.

'This is Buddy Whiffleflip, a forest pixie,' said Grace-Ella.

'Charmed to meet you,' said Buddy, bowing.

'He hid in my rucksack at Witch Camp and I'm letting him stay for a holiday.'

'But ... pixies ... aren't ... real,' stammered Fflur.

'I am most very real,' said Buddy. He hopped onto Fflur's lap. 'And I am most definitely a pixie.'

'You thought witches weren't real as well, remember,' said Grace-Ella with a giggle.

They were interrupted by a rustling and the cracking of twigs, followed by a sharp, 'Shhh.'

'Someone's here. Quick, get back in my bag.'

But before Buddy could move, out from behind a tree sprang Amelia and her friend Ceinwen.

'What are you two up to hiding down here?' Amelia demanded.

Grace-Ella glanced nervously at Buddy, who was sitting stone-still.

'It's none of your business,' she said. 'So why don't you buzz off to annoy someone else?'

'That's not very friendly, *Gross*-Ella,' Amelia smirked. She spotted Buddy on Fflur's lap. 'Oh look, how sweet. They're playing with dollies.'

'No, we're not,' snapped Grace-Ella.

'This is...'

She stopped. She couldn't tell the truth. Amelia would tell Mrs Nag and she would be in big trouble.

Amelia took a step closer. 'What an ugly-looking thing.'

Grace-Ella looked across at Buddy. His eyes were blazing fire-bright. She had never seen an angry pixie before. What was he going to do?

'Fflur and *Gross*-Ella play with dollies, little baby dollies,' sang Amelia. 'Just wait till I tell the rest of the class. Come on, Ceinwen.'

They turned to leave, but Buddy pounced and landed on the top of Amelia's head.

'Ugh! What's that?' she squealed, waving her arms wildly.

Grabbing her ears, Buddy pulled and Amelia started to lift off the ground.

'What's happening? Ceinwen, do something!' she screeched.

'I'll ... I'll go and get Mrs Nag,' squeaked Ceinwen, backing away, then running as fast as she could out of the school garden.

Amelia floated upwards into the apple tree, until she landed on one of the top branches. Buddy let go of her ears and bounced onto the branch next to her.

'You have a very nasty tongue. Pixies do not like spiteful sprites. And pixies do not like to be called ugly.'

Amelia stared at Buddy in disbelief. 'I don't know how you do these things, Grace-Ella, but get me down from here right now!'

'That is not the way to speak politely,' said Buddy. 'You can sit up here until you find your manners.'

'Grace-Ella! Get me down right now and get this ... this ... thing away from me!'

Grace-Ella couldn't help enjoying seeing Amelia stuck in the tree, but she began to worry that Buddy had been seen. How was she going to explain this away? Before she could think what to do, she heard voices drifting closer through the trees.

'If you've dragged me down here for nothing, Ceinwen, I will not be happy.'

Mrs Nag. A very cross-sounding Mrs Nag.

They came into view. Ceinwen whimpered, 'She ... she ... a creature got her.'

'Buddy, hide,' hissed Grace-Ella.

Before Buddy disappeared into her bag, Grace-Ella saw a sprinkling of his golden pixie dust shimmering on Amelia's hair.

'What is going on?' barked Mrs Nag, standing with her hands on her hips. 'Where's Amelia?'

'She's ... she's up in the tree.' Grace-Ella pointed.

Mrs Nag looked up. 'Amelia Cadwallader, get down this instant. We do not go apple scrumping at St. Winifred's.'

'I ... but...'

The pixie dust had made Amelia forget all about Buddy and what had just happened. She had no idea what she was doing up an apple tree.

'I'm stuck!' she wailed.

'Oh, what a palaver,' sighed Mrs Nag. 'Ceinwen, go and find Mr Broom and his ladder please.'

Mr Broom, the caretaker, arrived and

climbed up the ladder to help Amelia down.

'I'm very surprised at you, Amelia,' scolded Mrs Nag. 'Climbing up trees to scrump apples. What would your parents think?'

'But I ... I didn't climb...'

'Quite enough,' interrupted Mrs Nag. 'For the rest of the week, you can spend break times clearing up the garden. You can collect the edible apples in a basket for Mrs Bun to bake some pies, and throw the rotten ones onto the compost. Now back to the yard, all of you, before the bell rings.'

Amelia glowered at Grace-Ella, grabbed Ceinwen's arm and pulled her through the garden.

'Why did you go and get Mrs Nag? Because of you, I'm stuck with the stinky compost all week,' she snapped at her friend.

'But there was a creature in your hair,' said Ceinwen.

'I do not have creatures crawling in my hair, thank you very much,' retorted Amelia. 'If you say such a horrid thing again I won't be your friend and you won't be my partner for the Christmas Fair.'

With that she stomped off.

Making sure that Buddy was in her bag, safe from any more mischief-making, Grace-Ella turned to Fflur and smiled. 'Now that was magical,' she said.

Chapter Five
A Snooze, a Snore and an Open Door

Grace-Ella and Fflur were in the summer house, excitedly planning what they could make and sell on their Christmas Fair stall. They had been busy researching different charities and decided that if their stall won, they would donate the money from the Fundraising Flowerpot to *Coed Cadw* (the Woodland Trust). The school owned a small neighbouring field and the pupils had been brainstorming ideas for how it could be used. An assault course had been suggested, as well as an outdoor theatre for school performances. Grace-Ella and Fflur thought it would be the perfect place to plant a wildlife woodland.

'It would be wonderful to have our own

woodland,' said Grace-Ella. 'Just imagine – den-building, bug-exploring, campfire-cooking. Far more fun than sitting in the classroom all day.'

'We could make and sell our own Christmas cards,' suggested Fflur, 'using recycled card to raise awareness of cutting down trees and paper waste.'

'They could be Christmas cat cards,' added Mr Whiskins. 'I'd be willing to dress up as Santa Paws, just for you.'

Grace-Ella giggled. 'Now that I would love to see, but I think we need something more original than cards. A product that no one else will think of.'

They continued to ponder as Mr Whiskins and Buddy played catch with a pine cone.

'Pine cones are Christmassy,' said Fflur. 'Mam always has a basket of them on the table at Christmas. And they grow on trees, which fits perfectly with our charity. We could paint them as Christmas tree decorations.'

'That's a brilliant idea!' Grace-Ella beamed. 'And instead of just painting them, we could make them into pine-cone pixie decorations.'

'Perfect,' said Fflur clapping her hands. 'But we're going to need a lot of pine cones. How will we collect enough?'

'With a sprinkling of magic...' Buddy blew a puff of pixie dust into the air and a prickly pile of pine cones appeared in the summer house.

'I knew it was the best idea to let you stay,' said Grace-Ella.

The following morning Grace-Ella very firmly instructed Buddy to stay in her bag.

'However much I enjoyed seeing Amelia stuck up a tree, I think everyone needs a quiet day today.'

By the end of the first lesson, she hadn't finished that morning's reading test. Her mind kept drifting like a breeze-blown cloud, thinking about the wildlife woodland they could plant. She had to stay in to complete her test during break time. She worked as quickly as she could, worrying that Buddy wouldn't have time out of her bag if she didn't finish before the bell rang.

After answering the last question, she put down her pencil and puffed out a long breath. She looked at the clock on the wall. It was eleven o'clock! The bell should have gone fifteen minutes ago. Where was everyone? She looked out of the window and saw that they were still outside. Mrs

Nag very rarely gave extra break time, and certainly not when they were doing tests.

She peered into the corridor. All was quiet, no sign of any teachers. She crept out of the classroom. Passing the cloakroom, she glanced at her bag and groaned. It was gaping open! What was Buddy up to now?

She hurried to the staffroom to tell Mrs Nag that she had finished her test. She had to find Buddy before he played a prank on an unsuspecting pupil. She knocked on the door but there was no reply. When she pushed it open, the rhythmic sound of snoring drifted out of the room. Slouched in their chairs, the teachers were fast asleep.

The Fundraising Flowerpot was open on the coffee table next to Mrs Nag's raised feet. She must have been checking on the current total before nodding off. In the middle of the table was a glass bottle. She tiptoed over and read the label.

A special gift from me to you,
A thank you muchly for all you do,
So pour yourself a deliciousy cup,
Sit back, relax and put your feet up.

Grace-Ella sniffed the empty bottle. Lavender. She knew exactly who had left this special gift for the teachers... But where had he gone now?

Closing the door behind her, she decided to do a quick search inside first. She peered into the library. Everything was calm and quiet with no sign of any pixie mischief. Maybe he had found the cookery room and was happily munching on Mrs Bun's baked apple pies, she thought.

As she got nearer, Grace-Ella could hear clattering and banging and smell burning wafting down the corridor. This wasn't sounding or smelling promising. She burst through the door, but to her surprise, it wasn't Buddy she found, it was Amelia.

'Bother and blast! I'll never get them right,' said Amelia miserably as she dropped a smoking baking tray onto the worktop.

'What are you doing?' asked Grace-Ella.

Startled, Amelia quickly threw a tea towel over the tray. 'What are *you* doing creeping up on me? Trying to steal ideas for the Christmas Fair, no doubt.'

'No, I'm not. Fflur and I have a brilliant idea, actually. We don't need to steal anything,' retorted Grace-Ella.

'Well, go away then. I haven't got time to waste talking to you.' She looked up at the clock and gasped. 'Oh bothersome biscuits! I hadn't noticed the time. Did Mrs Nag send you? I'm going to be in big trouble now for being late to lesson.'

'Calm down. No one sent me. The teachers are fast asleep in the staffroom. Mrs Nag hasn't rung the bell for the end of break yet. Everyone is still outside. Well, everyone except you, that is. Why *are* you in here?'

‘None of your business, so go away,’ snapped Amelia.

Remembering that she was meant to be looking for Buddy, Grace-Ella left Amelia to whatever she was up to and headed outside to find Fflur. She knew she wouldn’t be in the garden as that was where Amelia was meant to be, clearing up apples. So she guessed that she would be in their secret spot behind the gym changing rooms. To her relief, Buddy was there too.

‘I hope you don’t mind that I took Buddy out of your bag,’ said Fflur. ‘I’ve been so excited to see him again.’

‘Of course I don’t mind. I need all the help I can get to keep him out of mischief! And speaking of mischief, Buddy, why are the teachers asleep?’

Buddy beamed. ‘You said that the teachers needed a quiet day, so I left them a bottle of your *deliciousy* Lullaby Lavender Lemonade. They can have a sleepy day and you can play.'

'Buddy Whiffleflip, what am I going to do with you?' said Grace-Ella, smiling despite her exasperation. 'I suppose it won't do any harm to leave them sleep for a little while longer. They could do with a rest.'

At half past eleven, she decided that they really should stir the teachers, otherwise there would be no lunch.

'You'll have to use your pixie dust to wake them, or they'll be asleep until home time.' She tucked Buddy inside her cardigan. 'Fflur, you keep watch and stop anyone from coming in.'

They shuffled quietly along the corridor towards the staffroom. The door was open.

'I definitely closed it.' Grace-Ella frowned.

She peered around the open door. The

teachers were still fast asleep but there was someone moving around in there – Amelia. She was gently shaking Mrs Nag.

'Mrs Nag? Mrs Nag? It's almost lunchtime. You need to wake up.'

Mrs Nag let out a loud snore.

'We'll have to wait for Amelia to leave,' whispered Grace-Ella. 'I can't let her see you again.' They ducked down beside the photocopier to wait, but Grace-Ella peeped round as much as she dared, so she'd know when Amelia was coming out.

Amelia tried to wake each teacher in turn. When it was clear that none of them were going to stir, she shrugged and turned to leave. Then she paused, staring at the coffee table.

Grace-Ella watched wide-eyed as slowly Amelia reached inside the Fundraising Flowerpot, clutched all the money and stuffed it into her pocket. She put the lid back on and screwed it shut.

Grace-Ella dived back into her hiding place beside the photocopier, just as Amelia closed the staffroom door behind her and ran down the corridor.

'I can't believe it!' whispered Grace-Ella. 'Amelia has stolen the fundraising money!'

Chapter Six
Carlo's Creations

'That's beastly bad, even for Amelia,' said Bedwyr.

Straight after school, Grace-Ella had asked him to meet her in the summer house. She had just told him all about Amelia stealing the money from the Fundraising Flowerpot. 'When Mrs Nag finds out the money is missing, she'll have us all in detention. She's sure to cancel the Christmas Fair and then we won't even get a chance to donate money to the Woodland Trust.'

'I shall put Amelia back in the apple tree until she learns to behave,' stated Buddy with a stomp of his foot.

Grace-Ella didn't think that sitting in an apple tree was going to help this time. She needed proof that Amelia had stolen the money so she could tell Mrs Nag.

'Well, I'm definitely up for some crime-busting instead of bug-busting,' said Bedwyr, snapping on his 'X-ray' swimming goggles. 'It's actually very exciting to have a criminal living amongst us.'

The four of them huddled together to form a plan: Grace-Ella and Bedwyr would wait and watch behind old Wini Watkins' hedge, opposite Amelia's house. Wini Watkins was about a hundred years old and very hard of hearing. She spent her days watching quiz shows, with the volume turned up to maximum. It was very unlikely that she would notice two children sitting under her hedge.

Buddy's job was to peek through the windows of Number 15 to see what Amelia was up to. If she left the house, then it was

Mr Whiskins' job to follow her.

As stealthy as spies, they climbed over the garden fence to the path at the back of the house. Once Mr Whiskins and Buddy had checked all was clear and Wini Watkins was shouting at the telly, Grace-Ella and Bedwyr climbed over her fence and crept round the side of the house.

The lights were on downstairs at Number 15. Amelia's dad's car wasn't on the driveway. He was the manager of the bank in Aberbetws and didn't usually get home from work until about 7pm.

'OK, Buddy. Go and see what you can find,' whispered Grace-Ella.

Buddy leaped onto Mr Whiskins' back and they bolted across the road, disappearing into the garden of Number 15. Grace-Ella and Bedwyr waited under the hedge.

‘Hey, what’s that?’ hissed Bedwyr.

‘What? Can you see her? What’s she doing?’ asked Grace-Ella.

‘Not Amelia. That bug. I think it’s an evil weevil.’

‘Bedwyr, you’re meant to be busting Amelia, not bugs.’

‘Sorry. There’s some binoculars in my bug-bag. See if you can see anything while I just catch this little weevil.’

Grace-Ella poked the binoculars through the hedge. Although the lights were on at Number 15, she was too far away to be able to see what was going on inside. She was about to hand the binoculars back to Bedwyr when a giant green eye appeared in the lens.

She screamed and toppled backwards, landing flat on her back on Wini Watkins’ driveway.

‘It’s only me,’ said Mr Whiskins, pouncing

over the hedge.

'You gave me a fright, creeping up on me like that.'

'I'm a spy-cat. I'm supposed to creep.' He looked around to check that no one

was nearby, then lowered his voice. 'I have important information.'

The important information was that Mrs Cadwallader was in a very peculiar pose on her yoga mat in the living room, and Amelia was in the kitchen, baking.

'She was baking at school during break time today as well,' said Grace-Ella. 'I never knew baking was her hobby.'

'Maybe she's doing some kind of charity bake-athon,' suggested Bedwyr, 'and she stole the money to look like she's raised more money than she actually has! I bet that's it! The sneaky snake!'

'If she was doing a charity fundraising thing, then everyone would know about it,' said Grace-Ella. 'She would have been talking about it non-stop. If there's one thing that Amelia likes, it's having all the attention on her.'

'This is fun, it's like solving a riddle,' said Buddy.

'It's definitely puzzling,' replied Grace-Ella. 'Amelia would never risk being expelled from St Winifred's. She would die of shame. There must be a really good reason for her to steal the money. She may be a horrible bully, but that doesn't mean she's a criminal.'

They were about to give up on their crime-busting for the evening, when they heard a van pull up outside Amelia's house. Grace-Ella pushed the binoculars through the hedge again. Painted on the van's side was a crumbling chocolate-chip cookie and a sparkling sprinkle-topped cupcake. In silver swirly letters were the words, 'Carlo's Creations.'

'It's from the new bakery in town,' said Grace-Ella. 'Dad was telling us about it

last week. He said that Carlo is an award-winning pâtissière and people from all over the country buy his cakes.'

They all peered over the top of the hedge. The front door of Number 15 flew open and Amelia came running down the path. Carlo, a very jolly, round man wearing a chequered apron and chef's hat, stepped out of the van.

'Delivery for Meez Amelia,' he said in his strong Italian accent. He handed her a white cardboard box.

Amelia grabbed the box and, balancing it under one arm, gave Carlo some money.

'Grazie, Meez Amelia. Enjoy Carlo's creations.'

Amelia hurried back into the house, slamming the door shut. The van drove away. The four spies watched until it turned the corner out of the Close and disappeared.

'Well, it looks like she took the money

to buy cakes from the new bakery,' said Grace-Ella. 'Dad did say that they cost a small fortune because Carlo is so famous. Maybe she wants to give her mam and dad a surprise present? Maybe it's their birthday or a special wedding anniversary or something?'

'Nah, I'm not buying that,' said Bedwyr. 'Amelia doesn't do nice things like surprise presents unless they're for herself. This is all very whiffy, if you ask me.'

'I agree,' said Mr Whiskins. 'There's something very fishy-kippers going on. I have a tingling in my tail.'

Grace-Ella sighed. It was all a muddle. Amelia had definitely stolen money from the school. But why? To buy cakes for her mam and dad? Or was there another reason?

And how was she going to find proof

before Mrs Nag found out the money had gone and cancelled the Christmas Fair?

Chapter Seven
Sugar and Spice

The following morning, Buddy decided to stay at home to mix up some pixie dust in the summer house. Grace-Ella was relieved – it was one less thing to worry about in school!

While they were working on their pine-cone pixie project, Grace-Ella told Fflur what had happened the previous evening.

'We'll have to watch her closely to see if she does anything unusual. There must be another reason why she stole the money, not just to buy some fancy cakes. If Mrs Nag finds out, she'll be expelled, and Amelia would never risk being kicked out of school.'

There had been no mention of the missing money from Mrs Nag. She had clearly been too flustered after waking up yesterday to look in the Fundraising Flowerpot. But she was sure to check the total before the Christmas Fair.

In the last lesson of the day, Mrs Nag asked every pair to present their idea for their Christmas Fair stall to the rest of the class.

Catrin and Aniela went first. They were painting small glass jars with Christmassy patterns, to be filled with sweet treats. Megan and Martha were making Christmas pomanders. They held up an orange with a red ribbon tied in a bow around it. The peel was studded with cloves in swirling patterns.

There were paper wreaths, salt-dough Santas, buttons-and-beads tree decorations and crafty cards. Grace-Ella and Fflur showed one of the pine-cone pixies they'd made and smiled proudly when Mrs Nag said that they were adorable and sure to be very popular.

The last pair to be called was Amelia and Ceinwen. Amelia was carrying a white cardboard box.

'Our stall is umm ... called ... umm ... Sugar and Spice,' she announced shakily.

That was strange – she wasn't being her usual confident and boastful self. And if Grace-Ella wasn't mistaken, she had a very shifty look about her, her eyes darting from Mrs Nag to the box and back again. After an elbow-nudge from Ceinwen, she opened the box and pulled out a glittery, cellophane-wrapped, snowman-shaped biscuit. 'We're umm ... baking … umm ... cinnamon-spiced snowmen.'

A gloriously mouth-watering scent filled the classroom. Fflur's stomach gave a very loud gurgle and everyone giggled.

'They look and smell absolutely divine,' said Mrs Nag. 'I'll definitely be buying a box or two. How wonderful to see you putting your cookery lessons with Mrs Bun to good use. Well done, the pair of you.'

As Amelia smiled her sickly-sweet smile, the puzzle-pieces slotted together in Grace-Ella's brain. That was why Amelia had stolen the fundraising money – she hadn't baked the biscuits herself, she had bought them from Carlo's Creations! What a cheat! Well, she wasn't going to get away with it.

'Mrs Nag,' called Grace-Ella, her hand shooting into the air.

'Yes, Grace-Ella?'

She was about to blurt out that Amelia had stolen the money from the Fundraising Flowerpot to buy the biscuits, but realised that she had absolutely no proof. Would

Mrs Nag believe her? Or would she think that she was trying to sabotage their stall because she was jealous?

'Well?' said Mrs Nag.

'Umm ... I just ... well ... the thing is...' She chewed her bottom lip. Everyone was watching her and she felt a beetroot bloom spread across her cheeks. 'Well, umm ... I was just wondering if … umm ... we can choose ourselves how much to sell our product for?'

'Of course. They're your stalls. You make all the decisions. This is an excellent opportunity for you to develop your entrepreneurial skills as well as your creative talents.'

'We're so going to win this,' said Amelia, skipping back to their table, her confidence restored. 'That trophy will definitely have our names on it.'

Later that evening, Grace-Ella was in her bedroom with Buddy and Mr Whiskins.

'How am I going to prove that Amelia stole the money and is cheating?' she asked miserably. 'I don't even think my magic can help this time. I have to find proof, real proof that I can show Mrs Nag. Then everyone will know what a sneaky snake she really is.'

In the morning, Grace-Ella decided that the only thing she could do was confront Amelia and demand that she confess.

'Do you really think she'll listen to you?' worried Fflur.

'I have to do something. She can't get away with stealing and cheating,' said Grace-Ella. 'You look after Buddy while I sort this out.'

She found Amelia and Ceinwen in the school garden. Amelia was sitting on the bench whilst Ceinwen was doing all the work picking up the windfall apples from the ground. Grace-Ella had fluttery butterflies in her belly, but she wasn't going to back down.

'I want to speak to you,' she said, stopping by the bench.

Amelia yawned exaggeratedly. 'If you must.'

Without pausing for breath, she blurted, 'I know you're lying and cheating and you stole money from the Fundraising Flowerpot to buy the snowmen biscuits from Carlo's Creations.'

Amelia shot up. 'What are you talking about?'

'I saw you steal the money and I saw Carlo delivering biscuits to your house. You're a thief and a cheat!'

Amelia glanced over at Ceinwen, who

was tipping rotten apples onto the compost and couldn't hear what was going on.

'How dare you accuse me of stealing,' spat Amelia. 'I baked those biscuits myself. I've been practising for days to get them just right.'

'You're lying,' said Grace-Ella. 'And I'm going to tell Mrs Nag.'

'You wouldn't dare! You're too much of a cowardy-cowpat.'

'I'm not a coward. You think you can get away with everything. Well, I'm not going to let you.'

'Fine,' sighed Amelia. 'Tell Mrs Nag. Oh, and remember to show her the evidence. I mean, you have got evidence, haven't you? Everyone knows you need evidence before accusing someone, but then I don't suppose your bat brain thought of that.'

Grace-Ella clenched her fists tightly.

Anger bubbled and brewed inside her like a boiling cauldron.

'Ha! I knew you didn't. Do you really think Mrs Nag will believe you?' snarled Amelia. 'Do you really think she'll believe that sweet little me would do such a thing?'

'Sweet? You're as rotten as the apples on the compost heap,' said Grace-Ella.

'Oh, look,' said Amelia, bending down to put apples in a basket. 'Mrs Nag's coming. You can tell her right now ... but remember, I'm the star at Saturday Stage School. I can make myself cry with the click of my fingers. I'll be dreadfully upset at your horrid lies.'

Grace-Ella was shaking. It was her word against Amelia's. If Amelia started sobbing and told Mrs Nag that she was saying nasty lies about her, then she would be the one in trouble.

‘Glad to see you carrying out your punishment, Amelia. And how kind of Grace-Ella and Ceinwen to help you,’ said Mrs Nag as she walked towards them.

‘Yes, Mrs Nag. They’re the best friends,’ replied Amelia. Putting on a sad face, she added, ‘I’m really sorry that I climbed the tree. I thought I saw a bird’s nest and I was worrying that there might be baby birds in it and that they would be cold over the winter. I wanted to ask if we could put some bird boxes up, so that they could shelter from the cold weather.’

‘How very thoughtful of you. Why didn’t you say so?’

‘I got scared once I was up the tree. I’m scared of heights and I think I was suffering from vertigo.’

‘Well, you needn’t have worried. Birds don’t nest at this time of year, but bird boxes are a wonderful idea,' said Mrs Nag. 'I'll tell Mr Broom and we'll have some put up in time for spring. And now that you've explained properly, I don't think you need to spend any more of your break times clearing apples.'

Mrs Nag strolled back through the garden. Amelia looked at Grace-Ella. 'What happened? Cat got your tongue? Come on, Ceinwen, let's leave *Gross*-Ella with the rotten apples. We've got posters to design for our winning stall.'

She linked her arm with her friend and strutted off. Grace-Ella felt tears pricking her eyes. Amelia was a thief and a cheat, but there seemed to be absolutely nothing she could do to prove it.

Chapter Eight
Truth Means Proof

As the pile of pine-cone pixies grew, so did Grace-Ella's frustration. There were only a couple of days left until the Christmas Fair and she was no closer to proving that Amelia had stolen the fundraising money.

'Can't you use your magic on her just this once?' asked Fflur, as they stitched and stuck scarves, hats and mittens for their pine-cone pixies. 'I'm sure the Witch Council wouldn't find out. They can't possibly know everything that goes on.'

'I can't risk it,' said Grace-Ella miserably. 'Imagine if they did find out and I had my magic taken from me. It would be the worst thing ever. Even worse than allowing

Amelia to get away with cheating.'

'I still think I should put her back in the apple tree,' said Buddy.

'Hmm ... yes ... something ... should be done,' muttered Bedwyr. He was busy looking for bugs in the folds of the pine cones with his magnifying glass and not really paying much attention.

'It's always best to think about things logically,' said Mr Whiskins. 'We know that Amelia has stolen the money to cheat at the Christmas Fair. When Mrs Nag finds out that the money is missing, she will cancel the Christmas Fair. And we will have a hundred homeless pine-cone pixies. Therefore Amelia needs to confess and give the money back so that the Christmas Fair can go ahead.'

'You make it sound very straightforward,' said Grace-Ella. 'But there is no way that

Amelia is going to confess. So looking at it logically, the Christmas Fair is doomed.'

Later that evening, Grace-Ella sat on her bed with her Witch Tablet. She opened the file 'Spelling Steps'. Now that she had received her 'Spells for Beginners' certificate at Witch Camp, she had to work her way through the nine 'Spelling Steps'.

Having been busy with Buddy's unexpected arrival, she hadn't had a chance to practise any of her new spells. She scrolled down the alphabetical list on Step One...

'That's it!' She leaped off the bed. 'I've found the perfect spell! Tell-It-True. A truth-telling spell! Truth means proof!'

'Yipee!' squealed Buddy with a flying flip.

'You are a magnifulous-splendifulous witch,' said Mr Whiskins.

Grace-Ella puffed with pride. 'Now that I have the right spell, I just need to find a way of casting it without breaking any of the Nine Golden Rules.'

At school, everyone was busy working on their projects. With the Christmas Fair only a day away, excitement buzzed around the classroom. Even Mrs Nag was humming happily as she marked their end-of-term tests.

Grace-Ella and Fflur were writing out instruction cards for how to make a pine cone pixie. Grace-Ella had just told Fflur about the Tell-It-True spell.

'I just need to find a way of casting it without breaking any rules. I can't wave my magic wand in front of everyone, because then I'd be breaking the first rule and be in big trouble with Mrs Nag at the same time.

And I can't cast it directly onto Amelia because I'll be breaking Rule Number 5 – never use magic on unsuspecting victims.' She blew out a long breath like a deflating balloon. 'It's so hard sticking to all the rules.'

'You cast the spell on the library at Halloween, not on Amelia, so you didn't break any rules,' said Fflur, remembering the flying books, swaying chandelier and flappy bats.

Grace-Ella was confident that her spell would work, but couldn't work out how and when to use it. There was a lot more to magic than just waving a wand around. If only it was that easy!

'Right, class,' said Mrs Nag. 'You've all worked extremely hard on your projects and I'm looking forward to seeing your work on show. Tomorrow afternoon you'll set up your stalls outside. There are two judges coming to the school – Miss Rose, the owner of the flower shop in Aberbetws, and Mr Madog, our Chair of Governors. They'll be judging your produce and your display – looking at creativity, originality and quality. They've prepared a questionnaire for you to fill in about how you came up with your idea, how you feel your project has gone and what skills you have learned. They will then make their decision after school, while having tea with the teachers. The Christmas Fair will open at six o'clock and the winning stall will be given their prize a little later in the evening, and we'll announce how much the Flowerpot Fund has raised!'

Grace-Ella glanced at Amelia. She was sitting still and upright, as calm as an empty cauldron. Grace-Ella felt furious sparks explode inside her. She wasn't going to let Amelia get away with stealing and cheating. She *had* to cast her spell before tomorrow evening. If Mrs Nag opened the empty Fundraising Flowerpot in front of a the whole school, it would be a disaster.

At that exact moment, Mrs Nag pulled the Flowerpot out from under her desk. Grace-Ella gasped. Mrs Nag was about to find out that the money was missing! Everyone's hard work would be wasted. It was too late for Grace-Ella to save the Christmas Fair.

Feeling utterly wretched, she watched as Mrs Nag pulled the lid off ... and pulled out a pile of money! Grace-Ella rubbed her eyes and opened them as wide as she could, to make sure that she wasn't seeing things. But no, Mrs Nag was definitely clutching the money and smiling at the class.

'Most of the money has already been banked, but this is the money that we raised during our friendly hockey match earlier this term. Let's count it out together...'

Grace-Ella couldn't believe it. How could the money possibly be back in the

Flowerpot? Her thoughts tumbled about like clothes in a washing machine as everyone counted along with Mrs Nag.

'Two hundred and thirty-five pounds. Added to the three hundred pounds that has already been put safely in the fundraising account, that's five hundred and thirty-five pounds. Along with the money from tomorrow evening, this will be a wonderful donation to the chosen charity.'

When the bell for home time rang, Grace-Ella walked quietly out of the classroom.

'I don't understand,' she said to Fflur. 'I saw her take the money. I swear I did.'

'I believe you. But she must have put it back.' Fflur shrugged. 'That's a good thing though, isn't it?'

'Amelia,' Mrs Nag called from the

classroom. 'Could you return the Fundraising Flowerpot to the staff room, please?'

Amelia strutted down the corridor. Like an angry wasp, Grace-Ella zipped after her. 'You put the money back. I know you stole it. I saw you.'

Amelia looked pityingly at Grace-Ella. 'The thing you don't understand, *Gross-Ella*, is that I have a brain for business and can think on my toes. I'm not a loser like you. And please get your facts right – I didn't *steal* the money. I *borrowed* it until I had my pocket money at the weekend. And then I put what I *borrowed* back in its rightful place on Monday morning. Borrowing is what businesses do. I should know. My dad *is* a bank manager.'

'But you're cheating,' said Grace-Ella. 'Everyone else has worked really hard to make their own product and all you've done is buy biscuits.'

'Like I said, I can't help it if I have a brilliant business brain.'

She skipped off, leaving Grace-Ella to stare furiously after her.

Well, Amelia might think she had a brilliant business brain, but Grace-Ella was a magnifulous-splendifulous witch. She had magic at the tips of her fingers and a spell to cast!

Chapter Nine
A Sniff and a Sneeze

Grace-Ella paced around the summer house, her magic wand held tightly in her hand. Mr Whiskins and Buddy watched her walk back and fore, to and fro, this way and that.

'I can't cast it directly on Amelia ... I need to cast it on something else ... something that can tell the truth ... something connected to Amelia...'

'What if you cast the spell on the snowmen biscuits?' suggested Buddy.

'I don't think talking biscuits will work,' said Grace-Ella. 'I suspect a talking biscuit would cause a lot of screaming and then we wouldn't be able to hear what they said anyway. It has to be something that won't look out of the ordinary. Something that can reveal the truth so there's no way that Amelia can wriggle out of it. It has to be there, in black and white...'

Grace-Ella stopped still. She slowly turned to face Mr Whiskins and Buddy, a smile twitching then stretching like elastic across her face.

'That's it! Black and white. Written down. The questionnaire. Answer true.' Grace-Ella's words tumbled from her mouth like a toppling tower. 'Sorry, I'm not making sense. What I mean is, I can cast the spell on Amelia's pen before she fills in the judges' questionnaire, and then her pen will write the truth. The truth will be there, right in front of the judges' eyes, in black and white.'

'*Purrr*fect,' purred Mr Whiskins.

'Pixie perfect,' agreed Buddy with a flippety-flip.

'It's still going to be a bit tricky to cast it without anyone noticing me.'

'Then it's lucky that you have a forest pixie,' said Buddy with a wink. 'You can cast your truth spell on my pixie dust, then sprinkle some on Amelia's pen and ... *poof*! You'll have the truth!'

'Brilliant!' squealed Grace-Ella. 'We make the best team. Let's do it.'

Buddy opened a pouch of his glittering golden pixie dust. Waving her wand, Grace-Ella said the magic words.

'Swizzle, swirl and sparkle bright,
This pixie dust will make things right,
Squiggle, scribble, doodle-do,
Write away and tell it true.'

A rainbow of sparkles flickered in the air, then sprinkled onto the pixie dust. Grace-

Ella tied the pouch with its golden ribbon and left the magic to settle overnight.

Friday was a flurry of activity. After lunch, everyone began to set up their stalls. Mr

Bevin had helped Grace-Ella to cut some thin, twiggy branches and spray-paint them silver. With a dark-green tablecloth peppered with a pot of artificial snow, clusters of wooden toadstools and a scattering of crisp-dry leaves, the 'Pine-cone Pixies' stall looked like a winter woodland. They hung the pixies from the silver branches and placed others amongst the toadstools to peek out at their customers.

'Are you sure your spell-dust is going to work?' asked Fflur.

'As sure as I have ten tiddly toes,' said Grace-Ella.

She pulled the pouch from her bag and untied the ribbon. The truth-dust glimmered a bright bluebell-blue.

'It's beautiful, isn't it,' she whispered.

Fflur peered into the pouch. 'Ooh, it's amaze ... ama...' She sniffed. 'It's a ... a ... ATISHOOOOOO!'

The truth-dust billowed out of the pouch and showered over the pine-cone pixies.

'Oh no!' gasped Fflur. 'What have I done? I'm so sorry. I forgot I have a dust allergy. You have got more, haven't you?'

Grace-Ella shook her head, staring at the shimmering blue scattered over their stall. That was it. Their chance of getting Amelia to tell the truth had been sneezed away.

She slumped into her chair.

'I really am sorry,' sniffed Fflur, sitting down next to her. 'You are still my friend, aren't you?'

Grace-Ella sighed then put her arm around Fflur's shoulders. 'Of course I'm still your friend. It wasn't your fault. It was an accident.'

'Can you make some more truth-dust? We could work out a way of using it this evening if we think really hard.'

'The spell has to be left to settle on the dust for a few hours to work properly. There isn't time,' answered Grace-Ella.

'What about casting your spell on Amelia? Then she might tell the truth herself?' said Fflur, desperately wanting to make things right.

'It's too risky,' said Grace-Ella. 'You know I'm not allowed to cast a spell directly on her without her knowing. Come on, let's get our stall finished, the judges will be here any minute. At least we still have a chance of winning and getting our wildlife woodland.'

Crouching down, Grace-Ella started to pin and hang the instruction cards for making a pine-cone pixie from the front of their stall. A movement on the table top caught her eye.

She stood and stared at their display but she couldn't see anything odd. Fflur had her back turned and was putting up the name of their stall on the awning above them. Shaking her head, Grace-Ella returned to the cards.

As she knelt down, she heard what sounded suspiciously like a pitter-patter of little feet. She slowly peeked over the edge of the table and gulped.

'Fflur? Fflur?' she hissed.

'What is it?'

'Look…!'

The pine-cone pixies were moving around on the table!

'What are they doing?' said Fflur, wild-eyed.

'It looks like my spell has started to work

on the pixies,' whispered Grace-Ella. 'It would have made Amelia's pen move by itself to write the truth ... so I think it's making the pixies move!'

Just then, one of the tiny pixies leaped from the table and scurried under the next stall: Amelia's and Ceinwen's.

'We can't let anyone see them,' panicked Grace-Ella. 'Quick, try to grab them.'

But with the spell now working fully, the pine-cone pixies began to scuttle and scoot in every direction. Grace-Ella and Fflur stared in horror.

'What in the world?' said Amelia, staring at their stall.

'Argh!' screamed Ceinwen as a pine-cone pixie scampered across her lap.

Within seconds, screams and shrieks filled the air as tiny pixies flitted and flipped and scuttled about everywhere.

‘What are we going to do?’ said Fflur, wobbly with worry.

Before Grace-Ella could answer, the double doors into the school flew open and out walked Mrs Nag and the judges...

Chapter 10

Pixie Pandemonium

'Girls, our judges have arrived...'

Mrs Nag froze. She stared unblinking at the chaos before her. There were children standing on chairs, cowering under tables and running around in a frenzied flock.

'Mrs Nag,' screeched Ceinwen, standing on her chair. 'Help!'

Mrs Nag didn't move, not even a twitch. A very red-faced Mr Madog stood on one side of her and a goggling Miss Rose on the other.

'What shall we do?' whispered Fflur. 'This is all my fault. We're going to be in so much trouble. Do you think our parents will be called in? Do you think we'll get expelled? Oh, Mam and Dad won't like this at all.'

'OK, stop worrying about all that

now,' said Grace-Ella, trying her best to keep calm. 'We'll have to deal with the consequences after. Let's try to catch all the pixies first and put them in my bag. Hopefully the magic will wear off soon.'

But it wasn't going to be easy to catch the little creatures. They were skittering and scurrying all over the place. It was pixie pandemonium!

Mrs Nag, regaining a little composure, marched into the middle of the fair. 'I have no idea what you all think you're doing, but I want you to stop right now. This is not how we behave at St. Winifred's.'

One of the pine-cone pixies chose that moment to scramble up Mrs Nag's trouser.

'What on earth...?'

Grace-Ella lunged, caught the little pixie and stuffed it into her pocket. 'We're very sorry, Mrs Nag. Umm ... you and the judges go and have a nice cup of tea ... and we'll ... umm ... all settle down and get back to our stalls.'

'There had better be a good explanation for this commotion,' hissed Mrs Nag. She ushered the two judges back inside to the staffroom, muttering an apology.

Grace-Ella raced around, swiping and snatching up pixies as swiftly as she could.

'Aw, they're so adorable,' said Aniela as she held a pixie in the palm of her hand. 'I want to keep one as a pet.'

'Sorry,' said Grace-Ella, grabbing the little pixie from her. 'You'll have to get a puppy or a parrot.'

'Phone pest control!' shouted Amelia on top of her table at the top of her voice. 'It's an infestation of rodents! It's like the plague!'

'Don't be so dramatic. They're not rodents,'

snapped Grace-Ella, as she rescued a pixie that was about to be stomped on by Amelia's shoe. 'They're just pine cones.'

There was a squeal from Martha. Grace-Ella had to hurry over and untangle a little pixie from her curly hair.

'Sorry, Martha,' she apologised. 'Pesky little things, eh!'

Grace-Ella dashed and darted around the stalls. Trying to catch a hundred wibbly-wobbly, roly-poly pine-cone pixies was proving impossible. With her pockets full, she ran back to their stall and tipped the pixies into her bag.

'Oof! Ouch!' came a muffled voice from inside. Out popped Buddy.

'I must have been dozing,' he said with a stretch and a yawn.

'Buddy! What are you doing here? I thought you were at home with Mr Whiskins,' said Grace-Ella.

'Cats are very lazy. School is much more fun than waiting for Mr Whiskins to stop snoozing. Is it playtime?'

'No, it isn't! It's pandemonium time!'

Buddy looked around, then peered into the bag at the jiggling pixies. 'It seems you have a pixie problem.'

'You could say that,' said Grace-Ella, zipping her bag closed before the little pixies escaped. 'The truth-dust got all over them and they've gone crazy! Can you help me catch them? Fflur, you stay with my bag and make sure they don't get out.'

Most of the girls had got over the initial shock of seeing rampaging pine-cone pixies and were having fun with them, scooping them up and watching them flip and fly out of their hands. Amelia was still on top of her table, shouting theatrically about fleas and disease, but no one was paying her any attention.

With everyone distracted by the pine-cone pixies, no one noticed the larger-sized, real-life pixie also running around. With Buddy's help, they managed to catch the rest.

Completely out of puff, Grace-Ella zipped

up her bulging bag. 'I think we've got them all.'

She glanced around. Now that there were no little pixies to play with, everyone was reluctantly straightening out and sorting their stalls, occasionally peering under their tablecloths and tables for any runaway pine cones. She was about to breathe out the biggest sigh of relief when she felt a sharp tap on her shoulder.

She turned and found herself nose-to-nose with Amelia.

'I think you have some explaining to do,' Amelia said, her hands on her hips. 'I think everyone would be very interested to know how your little pine-cone pixies CAME ... TO ... LIFE!'

Every pair of eyes was now on Grace-Ella. How was she going to get out of this? Was she going to have to tell everyone that she was a witch?

'We're waiting,' said Amelia impatiently.

'Umm ... well...'

'Grace-Ella does not have to speak to you,' said Buddy, kicking her in her shin. 'You are a spiteful sprite and a meanie maggot. Grace-Ella is kind and nice and should use her magic to turn you into an ugly old toad.'

A chorus of smirks and snorts, giggles and gasps, whispers and wonder echoed around the fair, as everyone tried to see who had spoken.

'How dare you speak to me like that, you horrid little thing!' raged Amelia. 'Look, everyone. Didn't I tell you at Halloween that Grace-Ella is not what she seems. Well, now you can all see for yourselves – she's a witch!'

Grace-Ella stepped out from behind their

stall and looked around at her classmates. Some were staring at her in awe, others were looking a little nervous.

'It's ... it's not like that,' she stuttered. 'It's just–'

'Don't say anything,' hissed Fflur. 'It's meant to be a secret, remember. You don't have to explain anything.' She turned to the other girls. 'You don't believe the nonsense that Amelia's spouting again, do you? Everyone knows there's no such thing as witches!'

'Of course there are wi–'

Grace-Ella gave Buddy a glare and a nudge with her foot to stop him saying any more.

'Witches are made up in stories. It was just a little technical hitch with our pine-cone pixies ... all to do with … umm ... faulty microchips and solar sun stuff,' said

Fflur. 'And anyway, we've got it all sorted now and the judges will be back any minute, so let's just get on with finishing our stalls. We all want to be the winner, don't we?'

Everyone seemed to accept Fflur's explanation and returned their attention to their stalls. Everyone except Amelia.

'Even better,' she snarled. 'You can explain all this in front of the judges.' She walked off.

'Thank you, Fflur. That was brilliant,' said Grace-Ella. 'Buddy, have you got your pixie dust? A sprinkling of your dust and everyone will forget all about what's happened.'

'Of course,' said Buddy. 'A pixie never goes anywhere without his dust.'

'Thank goodness,' said Grace-Ella, her relief blooming like a flower.

'But what about the truth-dust?' asked Fflur hesitantly. 'There isn't any left. We're not going to be able to prove that Amelia's cheating.'

'Ah! Then it's just as well that pixies bring good luck,' said Buddy, twinkling. He put his hand in his pocket and pulled out a golden pouch.

‘Is that what I think it is?’ said Grace-Ella.

‘If you are thinking that it is truth-dust, then you are thinking correctly. I was a teensy bit sneaky and scooped some into another pouch. I was going to use it on Morton, the magpie that lives in my oak tree. He keeps pinching my special golden ribbon but blames the squirrels.’

‘Buddy, I don’t care if you’ve been sneaky, you’re the best!’

Grace-Ella peeked into her bag. The pine-cone pixies were almost still. ‘Phew! It looks like the magic is wearing off. Right, let’s get these little pixies set out on the stall. I don’t think they’ll start rampaging around again. Buddy, you work your forget-me magic on everyone, including Mrs Nag and the judges. And as soon as I get a chance, I’ll sprinkle the truth-dust onto Amelia’s pen.’

Grace-Ella smiled. It finally looked like everything was going to plan.

Chapter 11
Tell It True

Ten minutes later, with Buddy's pixie dust having worked its forget-me magic, Mrs Nag and the judges walked out to find everyone waiting with excited anticipation behind their stalls.

'Right girls,' said Mrs Nag. 'The time has come. Our judges are here and can't wait to start judging your hard work. Mr Madog and Miss Rose will visit each stall and will give each pair a questionnaire to fill in. This evening we'll announce the winning stall, but I would like to say now that you're all winners in my eyes. You've worked very hard and this year's Christmas Fair will be an extra special one. I would like you to give yourselves a round of applause.'

As everyone clapped, Grace-Ella glanced

across at Amelia. She spotted her pencil case on the ground under their table. As soon as the judges were there, and Amelia's attention was fully on them, she would grab her chance and sprinkle the truth-dust.

'This is it,' said Fflur, as the judges headed towards their stall. 'Fingers crossed!'

'Hello, girls,' said Miss Rose. 'Would you like to introduce yourselves and your stall?'

'I'm Fflur and this is Grace-Ella, and our stall is called "Pine-cone Pixies".'

'Well, aren't these lovely,' said Miss Rose, holding one of the little pixies in her hand. 'You've clearly put a lot of work into them.'

Grace-Ella and Fflur smiled. If only she knew just how much work they had been!

'Oh, that tickled ... did it just move?' Miss Rose peered closely at the pine cone.

Grace-Ella sucked in a big breath. Was the magic dust still working?

'They're like wobbly weebles,' she said nervously as one of the pine cones on the table joggled and toppled over.

'Ha! Yes they are!' Miss Rose giggled. 'Well, I think they're charming.'

'Yes, excellent work, Grace-Ella and Fflur, I'm very impressed with your little prickly pixies,' said Mr Madog with a deep chuckle. 'If you could now fill in our questionnaire and all that's left for us to say is good luck!'

The judges moved over to Amelia and Ceinwen.

'That was close,' whispered Grace-Ella. 'Right, now's my chance to cast my spell.'

She pulled the pouch of truth-dust from her pocket and then knocked her pencil case off the table, scattering its contents everywhere.

'Oops, silly me!' she said, crawling on the ground to pick them up. With Amelia and Ceinwen paying her no attention, she stretched out her hand and sprinkled the truth-dust onto Amelia's pencil case.

'Fingers crossed this works,' she said, sitting down next to Fflur.

They began to fill in their questionnaire together. Amelia was holding out a plate for the judges to taste a sample cinnamon-spiced snowman, and it was clear from their faces that they were delicious.

Once the judges moved on to the next stall, Amelia snatched the questionnaire and grabbed her pencil case.

'I'll fill this in,' she said to Ceinwen. 'My handwriting is much neater than yours. And as I'm the one who baked the biscuits, I'll know the answers.'

She pulled a pen from her pencil case...

Grace-Ella's heart thud-thudded as she watched...

Amelia read the first question and began to write. A few minutes passed and nothing out of the ordinary seemed to be happening. Grace-Ella felt fidgety. She tapped her fingers on the table and her legs jiggled. Had the truth-dust worked?

When she was beginning to think it hadn't, Amelia's hand began to quiver and a frown formed on her forehead. Grace-Ella watched closely. Amelia's eyes widened in

surprise as her pen twizzled and twirled and took on a life of its own.

'Ceinwen,' she hissed. 'Something's wrong.'

Ceinwen looked at the paper. 'What are you doing? Why are you writing that?'

'I don't know,' Amelia replied, her eyes wide with woe.

'Well, stop it then! Why are you saying that Carlo baked the biscuits and you bought them from him? You'll have us disqualified. Write it properly!'

But Amelia had no control over her tell-it-true pen. She grabbed her right wrist with her left hand and tried to grapple the pen free, but it was no use. Word after word, sentence after sentence, the pen scribbled away.

'Cheating!' squeaked Ceinwen. 'Why are you writing that the skill you've learned is cheating?'

'Because it's all true,' said Amelia, her voice trembling.

'What do you mean?' asked Ceinwen. 'You said you baked them yourself! You said that you practised and practised until you got them perfect!'

'I did practise but I kept burning them. We never would have won the trophy with my biscuits. And then the idea just came to me: to buy them.'

'That explains why you wouldn't let me come over to help,' huffed Ceinwen. 'I can't believe you've done this. You've ruined our chance of winning.'

'Well, you didn't come up with a better idea…'

'Don't blame me for this!' shouted Ceinwen. 'This is all your fault!'

Grace-Ella heard every word. Mrs Nag too had noticed the squabbling happening on the 'Sugar and Spice' stall and walked briskly over.

'Is everything OK?' she asked.

'Umm ... yes, thank you, Mrs Nag,' answered Amelia, placing her hands over the questionnaire.

'No, everything isn't OK,' said Ceinwen, who was furious with her friend. 'Amelia has cheated.'

She grabbed the questionnaire and handed it to Mrs Nag. Mrs Nag scanned through the questions. Her nostrils flared and she pursed her lips.

'You have some explaining to do,' she said sharply. 'Staffroom, please. Now.'

As Amelia and Ceinwen left, Mrs Nag asked Mrs Bun, who was busy preparing the evening's refreshments, to take charge of the fair.

'That went perfectly,' said Grace-Ella

grinning. She grabbed the questionnaire and read the answers. 'It's all here – that Amelia bought the biscuits from Carlo's Creations, that she has no idea what the recipe is and that her best skill is cheating.'

'Does she say she stole the money?' asked Fflur.

Grace-Ella flicked through the questionnaire. 'No, she hasn't written that.'

'Are you going tell Mrs Nag?' said Fflur.

Grace-Ella placed the questionnaire back on the table. 'Do you know, I don't think I am. I mean, she did put the money back, so although it was wrong of her, technically it was borrowing, not stealing. We all do things without thinking sometimes. And there's no way that Mrs Nag is going to let her win now that she knows she's cheated. Not standing on the stage with the trophy in her hands and having to cheer for someone else will be the biggest and best punishment for Amelia. And I think it's going to take a lot of begging to get Ceinwen to forgive her this time. I think her *borrowing* can stay our secret.'

'You are the bestest and kindest witch,' said Buddy, peeking out of Grace-Ella's bag.

Chapter 12
Three Cheers for Trees

That evening, the school hall was a hub of Christmas merriment. The stalls had been taken inside now and the children were busy, proudly selling their Christmas produce to the parents. The 'Sugar and Spice' stall was now the 'Tea and a Tasty Bite' table, with Amelia and Ceinwen, alongside Mrs Bun, serving tea and coffee, apple pies and cinnamon-spiced snowmen biscuits to the parents.

At 7.30pm, Mrs Nag made her way onto the stage. She turned on the microphone, which crackled and gave an ear-piercing screech, and the hall fell silent.

'So, the big moment of the evening has arrived. I'm sure you'll all agree that our "Excellent Entrepreneur" project has been a great success. The girls have worked brilliantly together, delegating tasks, developing their business brains and using their creative talents to make their wonderful produce.'

Everyone gave a round of applause.

'Now, before I invite our judges to the stage to announce the winning stall, I can tell you that with your wonderful generosity this evening, the grand total of this year's Fundraising Flowerpot is a fantastic one thousand pounds.'

The hall once again erupted into rapturous applause. Everyone was thrilled with the amount raised.

'Please welcome onto the stage our judges, Mr Madog and Miss Rose.'

After once again thanking everyone for their hard work and the parents for being such enthusiastic shoppers, Mr Madog was ready to reveal who they had chosen to be the winning stall.

'In third place is "Buttons and Beads" by Rhiannon and Tia. Please come up to the stage to collect your certificate from Miss Rose.'

Rhiannon and Tia walked onto the stage to whoops and cheers.

'In second place is "Jolly Jars" by Catrin and Aniela.'

Once Catrin and Aniela had collected their certificates, a hush fell over the hall. Who was going to be the winning pair?

'And so we have our number one stall...' said Mr Madog. 'Miss Rose and I were very impressed with the originality and attention to detail of this produce and we're very happy to announce that the "Excellent Entrepreneur" trophy goes to ... Grace-Ella and Fflur for their wonderful "Pine-cone

Pixies" stall.'

Grace-Ella and Fflur felt like they were floating onto the stage. Mrs Bevin dabbed her eyes and Mr Bevin gave a double thumbs-up to Grace-Ella. Fflur's mam, Mrs Penri, clapped and whistled. Grace-Ella and Fflur held the glass trophy, smiling the widest smiles possible.

'Now, we are all looking forward to finding out to which charity you would like to donate this year's Fundraising Flowerpot,' said Mrs Nag. 'If you can step up to the microphone and tell everyone which charity you've chosen and why.'

Fflur held onto the trophy as Grace-Ella stood in front of the microphone.

'We would like to donate the Fundraising Flowerpot to the Woodland Trust. We would love to be able to plant trees in the field next to the school to create our own wildlife woodland. Trees are very important to our planet. They remove polluting gases from the air and provide safe habitats for wildlife. Planting just one tree can make a big difference and we want St Winifred's to be a part of that difference.'

Grace-Ella blushed crimson as everyone applauded.

'What a wonderful choice, girls. St Winifred's will be very proud to play a small part in helping our planet. And I think that planting our own wildlife woodland is a splendid idea. Let's give three cheers for trees!'

'It all worked out perfectly in the end,' Grace-Ella said to Mr Whiskins and Buddy, when they were all back at home. 'I'm so excited about having our very own wildlife woodland.'

'You should be very proud,' said Mr Whiskins. 'You're a magnifulous-splendifulous witch.'

'Well, I have had more than a helping hand from you, Buddy,' she laughed.

'I've had a hippy-hoppy-happy-holiday,'

said Buddy with an extra, extravagant flippety-flip. 'But I suppose it's maybe time for me to go back to Fir Tree Forest? I do have very important work to do and my forest friends will be missing me terribly.'

'Oh.' Grace-Ella suddenly felt sad. 'Of course. I mean, I would love you to stay here, it's been so much fun having you around. But I suppose a forest pixie needs to be in a forest. And you can come here on holiday any time you want.'

'As long as it's not too often,' added Mr Whiskins with a teasing twirl of his tail.

'Pixie-promise,' said Buddy.

'But how are we going to get you back home?' asked Grace-Ella. 'Mam and Dad don't know you're here, so I can't ask them to give you a lift. I'll have to send Penelope Pendle a message. I hope she won't be annoyed that I let you stay.'

'No need to worry,' said Buddy. 'I know just how to get back. My friend, Horatio Hoot the owl, will come and collect me.'

'You will stay till Monday though, won't you?' asked Grace-Ella. 'We're going to be planting the first trees in our new woodland and I think you should be guest of honour ... a hidden guest of honour, of course!'

On Monday morning, the whole of St Winifred's buzzed with excitement. Bethan Beech from the Woodland Trust came to their assembly to collect the fundraising cheque and to give a talk about their work.

'I am absolutely delighted to be here with you today,' she said. 'On behalf of the Woodland Trust, I would like to thank Grace-Ella and Fflur for choosing to donate your Fundraising Flowerpot to us. Our work is a means of setting roots for future generations to enjoy this wonderful planet that we live on. We plant trees, we restore ancient woodlands and we strive to protect wildlife. I'm looking forward to working with you here at St Winifred's to help you plant a new wildlife woodland.'

A presentation of the charity's work was shown. Bethan Beech explained how they were going to set about designing, creating and planting St Winifred's wildlife woodland. They spent the rest of the morning choosing which species of trees would be best, and learning how they would be planting their trees and how they would need to protect them once they were in the ground.

After lunch the first trees were delivered. Each pupil had their own sapling tree to plant. As it had been Grace-Ella's and

Fflur's idea, they would be the first to plant their saplings at the opening to the woodland.

With their trowels, they set about digging holes. Bethan Beech was busy showing Mrs Nag where the other trees would be planted. Grace-Ella opened her bag and out hopped Buddy.

'We couldn't plant the first tree without you here,' she said.

'Wait a second,' said Buddy, taking a pouch of pixie dust from his pocket.

'Oh no ... is that what I think it is?' asked Fflur, taking a step back.

'Yes, so don't come too close. We don't want another sneezy disaster,' said Grace-Ella.

Buddy poured the dust into the hole. Grace-Ella took her magic wand out of her bag and said the magic words.

'Sprinkle softly in the ground,
As birds sing sweetly all around,
Press down the roots and count to three,
A magic golden tree you'll see.'

'You're planting a magic tree?' asked Fflur excitedly.

'Of course,' said Grace-Ella. 'I mean, a woodland is a magical place after all.'

With Mrs Nag and Bethan Beech heading back towards them, Buddy hopped back into the bag.

'Well, girls,' said Mrs Nag. 'Now that we're going to have our very own woodland, it needs a name. I'm going to allow you to name it. You can have a think and get back to me when you've come up with one.'

'We already have a name,' said Grace-Ella. 'We would like to call our wildlife woodland The Golden Grove.'

'How wonderful,' said Bethan Beech. 'You're going to have lots of golden opportunities for learning out here.'

Grace-Ella smiled and behind her, her magical pine tree shimmered golden in the winter sunshine.

How To Make a Pine-cone Pixie

You will need:

- ★ A large pine cone
- ★ Coloured felt
- ★ Needle and thread
- ★ A large wooden bead
- ★ A small bell
- ★ A fine-tipped black marker pen
- ★ Scissors
- ★ Glue
- ★ Card

1) Draw an outline for a pair of mittens and a scarf on the card. Draw a heart-shape outline for your pixie's feet. Draw a triangle for your pixie's hat.

2) Cut the shapes out of coloured felt.

3) Glue the wooden bead onto the top of the pine cone.

4) Glue the felt feet to the bottom of the pine cone.

5) Sew the felt triangle to create a cone for the hat.

6) Sew the bell to the top of the cone hat.

7) Glue the hat onto the wooden bead.

8) Glue the felt mittens onto the pine cone.

9) Tie the scarf around the top of the pine cone and glue to keep it in place.

10) Draw a face onto the wooden bead.

A perfect pine-cone pixie!

At Firefly we care very much about the environment and our reponsibility to it. Many of our stories involve the natural world, our place in it and what we can all do to help it, and us, survive the challenges of the climate emergency.

Go to our website **www.fireflypress.co.uk** to see some of our great environmental stories.

We are always looking at reducing our impact on the environment, including our carbon footprint and the materials we use, and are taking part in UK-wide publishing initiatives to improve this wherever we can.

In *Pixie Pandemonium*, Grace-Ella and Fflur raise money for the Woodland Trust, which is a wonderful charity that works to protect, create and restore woodland across the UK.

To find out more about the Woodland Trust and their work, all details are on their website: **www.woodlandtrust.org.uk**